Donald Currie

Thoughts Upon the Present and Future of South Africa, and Central and Eastern Africa. A Paper Read by Donald Currie, esq., C.M.G., at the Royal Colonial Institute, on Thursday, 7th June, 1877

GW01057425

outlook

Donald Currie

Thoughts Upon the Present and Future of South Africa, and Central and Eastern Africa. A Paper Read by Donald Currie, esq., C.M.G., at the Royal Colonial Institute, on Thursday, 7th June, 1877

Reprint of the original, first published in 1877.

1st Edition 2024 | ISBN: 978-3-38555-723-9

Verlag (Publisher): Outlook Verlag GmbH, Zeilweg 44, 60439 Frankfurt, Deutschland
Vertretungsberechtigt (Authorized to represent): E. Roepke, Zeilweg 44, 60439 Frankfurt, Deutschland
Druck (Print): Libri Plureos GmbH, Friedensallee 273, 22763 Hamburg, Deutschland

THOUGHTS UPON THE PRESENT AND FUTURE OF SOUTH AFRICA, AND CENTRAL AND EASTERN AFRICA.

A PAPER

READ BY

DONALD CURRIE, ESQ., C.M.G.,

AT THE

ROYAL COLONIAL INSTITUTE,

On Thursday, 7th June, 1877.

His Grace The DUKE OF MANCHESTER, K.P.,
(President of the Institute), in the Chair.

LONDON.
1877.

THOUGHTS UPON THE PRESENT AND FUTURE OF SOUTH AFRICA, AND CENTRAL AND EASTERN AFRICA.

By Donald Currie, Esq., C.M.G.

A few days before the last meeting of the Members of the Institute, the Honorary Secretary, accompanied by a member of the Council, called upon me to explain the circumstances under which you had been disappointed in the arrangements you had made for a paper upon South Africa; and in the emergency it was pressed upon me that I might render a service, and further the object in view, by taking up the subject. I mention this at the outset, because it may be a matter of surprise to some of the Members present that I should appear here, having no claim whatever to a special knowledge of the subject, never having been in that country. But it seemed to me to be of great importance to the Cape Colony and Natal, to Griqualand and the Orange Free State, as well as to the Transvaal under present circumstances, and, indeed, to the whole of Southern, Central, and Eastern Africa also, that the affairs of that continent, and its probable future, should have the attention of the public by means of an enlightened discussion. You

A 2

will, therefore, bear with me, if in a somewhat
crude manner, and in the necessarily brief limits
of this paper, I deal with the principles which
affect that country, rather than with mere details,
which can be better insisted upon by those who
have lived in South Africa, and are conversant
with its special characteristics. The question is,
what combination of circumstances and systematic arrangement of means, what development
of resources and of motive power, is to press South
Africa forward in civilization and prosperity? And
in making these enquiries it will naturally occur to us
to bear in mind the obstacles which have hitherto
hindered a more complete success, and some of which
cannot be altogether removed.

I need not go back to the early history of
the Cape Colony and Natal. You all know how
the Dutch settlers, after the Portuguese discov-
eries, established themselves in the Cape Colony,
and subsequently in the interior and in Natal,
and how, by conquest and settlement, English
influence predominated. The history of the
establishment of the Orange Free State, and of the
Transvaal Republic, is sufficiently recent to be
well known to all interested in that part of the
world. I take as my starting point 1871, when responsible Government was given to the Cape Colony.
From that date the new history of South Africa
begins, with the political changes in the old Colony,

and the outcome of mineral wealth in the Diamond
Fields, followed by the dispute between the Imperial
Government and the Orange Free State. The
thoughts which occur to me in relation to these subjects
I propose very briefly to place before you ; they
may be taken as offering the texts for argument
and discusssion, and will, I am sure, have considerate
criticism.

Her Majesty the Queen, in 1871, upon the
recommendation of the late Government, gave to the
Cape Colony the power to control its own affairs.
By a small majority of the Cape Legislature this
privilege was accepted; but in the minds of many
throughout the Colony there prevailed the doubt
whether the Cape was sufficiently advanced to
undertake the duties of responsible Government.
In the Parliaments immediately preceding the
date of this establishment of virtual independence,
men then well known, but now still more
eminent, assisted to influence or direct the affairs
of the Cape Colony. The Honorable J. C. Molteno,
Prime Minister of the Cape, was then an inde-
pendent advocate for its liberties ; while the
distinguished chief of the Orange Free State, his
Honor President Brand, held his part in the
debates of an Assembly of which his father was the
Speaker. It is quite possible that those who then
objected to the capacity of the Cape Colony to manage
its own affairs might have been entitled to argue that

a postponement for a certain period would have been advisable; but now in this month of June, 1877, after the troubles and disputes connected with Confederation, and the Diamond Fields, and the Transvaal, I put it to you whether it is not good for South Africa that the Queen at that time gave the Cape Colony responsible Government? I venture to think that the prospects of to-day for the whole of South Africa would not have been so bright if the Imperial sanction had not been accorded to the natural instinct of Englishmen for self-government; and it will be admitted that the circumstances of the last five years have been favorable to a successful development of the principle of self government.

The South African communities, in the swift strides which they have made within the last few years, owe much of their intellectual and material progress to the influences of favorable circumstances. The discovery of diamonds in Griqualand West gave an impulse to the prosperity of South Africa. Hidden treasures of wealth were brought to light; fortunes were made; enterprise was stimulated; imports and exports were encouraged; immigrants were drawn to the country; land rose in value; and South Africa got a name. But then troubles arose. The acceptance of the cession of the Diamond Fields in the name of Her Majesty's Government opened up the question of the right to possess them. The Orange Free State claimed, with earnest indignation, that the land was theirs, and they stated they were prepared to prove their title to it. Controversy stimulated enquiry, and men's minds were naturally directed to the consideration of the question of what was right, and ought to be done.

To anyone acquainted with the politics of the Cape Colony, and the strong feeling which prevailed in the Orange Free State from 1871 until this question was settled, it is unnecessary to enter into details. There was everywhere amongst the men of Dutch descent, and amongst some Englishmen too, both in the Republics and in the Cape Colony, the belief that England was open to the imputation of having sought to possess what was not clearly proved to be within the just right of this country. All this, however, is now changed ; for the Orange Free State, upon the invitation of the noble Lord who directs the policy of the Colonial Office, deputed President Brand to visit England, and in due time the dispute was settled, with a generous and liberal regard for the rights of the Orange Free State. That State is satisfied; the Diamond Fields question is at rest. But the influence of the diamonds as a source of wealth, and of the Diamond Field question first as a subject of controversy, and afterwards as resulting in an honorable settlement, must be taken into account as of great importance in estimating all that affects the present and the future of South Africa.

In the Republic of the Transvaal, President Burgers—whose name I must always mention with respect, as one with whom I had the most intimate relations when he lived with me in England— had, up to the time of leaving his country to visit Europe, exerted in the short time which had elapsed after his election, the influence of an educated mind. But while giving Mr. Burgers credit for the utmost readiness to further a beneficent policy, such as that of the English Government towards South Africa, I must admit that on his return to the Transvaal after the successful settlement, as he thought, of the Loan in Holland, he evinced a desire to inaugurate efforts for Transvaal development which his country had not the means to accomplish.

A different policy prevailed in Natal. There the limited population of the subjects of the Queen, warm in the enthusiasm which they have as such, and courageous at the same time in the presence of an overwhelming force of savage tribes, thought less of aggrandizement and more of progress and development. And so it came to pass that her Majesty's Government settled with Natal the basis of a Railway system, which will materially contribute to the prosperity of that Colony.

What of Griqualand West, placed all along in a position of apparent antagonism with the Orange Free State ; treated with some indifference

by the Cape Colony; and burdened with a heavy
taxation in maintaining an administration of its own?
What could Griqualand West do although it possessed
a mine of diamonds? And what is to be the future of
Griqualand West? Through the action of the Home
Government and the enlightened accord of the Cape
Parliament, that part of South Africa will now have
its fortunes attached to the Cape Colony.

If it had not been for these vexed questions the
proposed confederation policy might have had a warmer
welcome in South Africa, and have met with less opposition; yet even now the Orange Free State is understood to have objections to the union of the states of
South Africa. President Brand did not feel it within
the scope of his powers to discuss the question at the
Conference with respect to native law and other
matters which was held in London last year, although
he concurred in the desirability of a common system of
police, the regulation of the sale of arms and of
spirituous liquors, as well as the development of industrial education; but time works wonders, and now that
the Transvaal has been annexed, it is very possible
that the people of the Free State will gradually
accustom themselves to the idea of a closer union
with the English Colonies. So long ago as the 22nd
December, 1858, the Orange Free State passed this
resolution:—" This Raad is convinced that a union
" or alliance with the Cape Colony, whether on
" the basis of federation or otherwise, is desirable,

" and therefore resolves to request his Honor the
" President to correspond with his Excellency the
" Governor upon that subject . . . . . for the
" purpose of planning the approximate terms of
" union."

In 1871 the Cape appointed a Commission on
Federation, and in their Report the following words
occur :—" Some, whose opinions are entitled to great
" respect, are of opinion that until the Free State,
" the Transvaal Republic, and Natal shew a disposi-
" tion to federate with the Cape, and until West
" Griqualand and the country between the Kei and
" the Bashee, or between the Kei and Natal, shall
" have been annexed to the Colony, no change of the
" kind proposed will be either necessary or expedient.
" . . . . The time may come when the advantage
" of a union among South African communities for
" the creation of a strong Government, powerful to
" protect, and, to a certain extent, to control its
" several members, will become apparent to all "—
while, in 1875, Natal and Griqualand West passed
resolutions that it was desirable to form a federative
union. Now that the Transvaal is joined to the
English possessions, there remains outside the Orange
Free State only, and her interests and sympathies
will bring her in; but time must be given for this,
and for the development of kindlier feelings than
those which prevailed during the Diamond Fields
dispute.

Here, then, in South Africa are several communities, all divided; all with special peculiarities; the Cape Colony itself actually, as is said by some persons, wishing to be divided into an Eastern and Western Colony; but whether one Colony or two Colonies, making up with the other parts of South Africa an assemblage of peoples who are kept separate now, not by conflicting interests, but by geographical and accidental conditions, by an unwillingness to face sudden political changes, and by misapprehension.

What systematic arrangement of means, what development of resources, is to press them all forward in union, civilization, and prosperity? Is each Colony, or State, to go alone? What will they gain by that? Or are they to unite into one great community for the general good of Africa, spreading fruitfulness, wealth, and happiness in their onward progress? And here, I may ask, what is there more fitting than the admirable words used by the noble Lord, who more than all others has sought to promote Colonial interests. In his speech in the House of Lords on the occasion of his introducing the Government Bill for the Confederation of the States of South Africa, Lord Carnarvon said:—" But of all the changes " which this measure may produce, I anticipate, " with the advent of political and administrative " union, none more hopefully than a real union in " sentiment of the Dutch and English race. The

" old quarrel to which I have alluded is dying out,
" is fast becoming a thing of the past : real
" friendliness exists under the crust of political
" discord . . . . . . all must gain in general
" political strength, as in material prosperity, by
" combination, and I will only add that my highest
" object has been to restore the union of sentiment
" between the two peoples."

A short time ago it was unpopular to say a word
in favour of Confederation; it might be better to call
it union, or community of interests ; but whatever
the name, the thing itself is now more acceptable.
I daresay, if Mr. Froude had stated that Lord Carnarvon only wished South Africa to be united and
prosperous, and that representatives should meet and
discuss its future, people there would have said this
was reasonable and good. But it was called Confederation, the proposed meeting was termed a Conference,
and when catch words are got hold of, misconceptions
are apt to follow. I venture to say that the position of
South Africa at the present moment warrants in the
minds of all, even of those who may not entirely agree
with the Colonial policy referred to, a cordial approval
of the statesmanlike prescience which can estimate
circumstances, and foresee and direct to a suitable
and satisfactory result.

Six months ago the Transvaal was at war with
Secocoeni, but now this chief is quiet; Cetchwayo, the
Zulu King, has withdrawn his warriors from the

borders of the territory ; and the British flag flies
over Pretoria. The people of the Transvaal did
not yield unwillingly to a manifest destiny when
they accepted with generous welcome the control of
a Government which now-a-days in South Africa is
so unlike the inconsiderate British rule of former
times. In that country, as in the Free State, the
recollection of a policy which could establish the
freedom of the slave, while disregarding the just
claims of the masters, and which, as in the case
of the Basuto war, could step in just at the moment
of the Boers' victory to secure our own supremacy
after we had parted with the Orange Free State as a
possession, could have had no friendly issue, if it had
not been for the wide-spread conviction that England
is now desirous to act justly and earnestly for the good
of South Africa. Who that knows the history of South
Africa can avoid regret and shame in the recollection that
when the slaves were set free the colonists were com-
pelled to discount their treasury bills, received as com-
pensation, at a ruinous loss, to colonial speculators, who
were also able to purchase the lands of the discontented
proprietors to great advantage, while the old owners
passed over the Vaal and Orange River to be free
from foreign control ?

We must all rejoice that the Transvaal is now
under British influence. That State is placed as a
wedge in the Southern part of Central Africa. With
Natal it controls the whole outlet to the north,

alongside of the Portuguese possessions on the coast line, and the future of the Transvaal will be closely identified with the future of Central Africa.

Amongst the influences which are to affect the future of South Africa, I think the first to be mentioned is Education. Already in the Cape Colony, and in the Free State and Natal, Colleges and Educational Institutions afford advantages to the rising generation. Institutions which I am told have in them the elements of future greatness, although more modest in administration than those which we possess at home. The facilities for travel place us here in contact from day to day with gentlemen from that distant country, who never before had seen England, or enjoyed its privileges; and I think it must be generally admitted that for intelligence and readiness of resource, the visitors from South Africa may bear comparison with any of us. Perhaps the climate has much to do with the quick perception and energy which are observed in the visitor from Africa, and under favourable circumstances the benefits of education will develope these and other qualities into higher intellectual power. In this I see for South Africa the source of great advancement, for if the climate of a country deadens or over-stimulates, how can we expect progressive and increasing prosperity? The white inhabitants of South Africa require their acutest faculties in dealing with the natives. They have not merely to place their colour in opposition to

the native people, they have to match intellect
against craft ; but if the South African is
destined to have the overwhelming superiority which
follows right dealing, and high moral influences, am I
not right in placing the highest education of the
intellect of South Africa as a most potent influence
for good in that land?

And then we must have Enterprise: and in the
word enterprise I include both mental and material
enterprise, under the influence of a fitting education,
that is to say, all that can advance sound christian
principles. It is a singular fact that while the hunter
in search of sport may have penetrated far into the
regions of Africa, or the trader in the pursuit of gain
has risked his life in its wilds, both have found far
ahead of them, at the utmost limits, the missionary
with the Gospel of Peace. And although this
is a topic which sometimes provokes a smile,
for I cannot but admit that there may occa-
sionally have been some unfitness in the agency
employed, yet it is not to be denied that
by a Moffatt, a Livingstone, and a Stewart in
Africa, or a Henry Martyn or Bishop Heber in India,
the conviction has been established that justice,
enlightenment, and high principle, govern the conduct
of our countrymen. But if it be conceded that these
principles must influence and prevail, I may take
it for granted that enterprise, missionary or commercial, will have the spring of enlightened earnest-

ness, and that the trader, or miner, or agriculturalist, like the missionary himself, will be impelled by something more than a mere love of gain.

Here I may remind you of the missionary and commercial zeal illustrated by the establishment of the Scottish and English Missions, as an advanced inland post of British influence amongst the natives on Lake Nyassa. The object there is to form a power for good, evangelical and industrial, designed to be a nucleus of advancing christian life and civilization to the Nyassa and surrounding region. It is a bold step: it is the most advanced effort in that quarter, and it has the character of nationality, for it places the English name on that inland sea as a point to which British influence must reach. The impression will arise in the minds of those who desire to honor the memory of Dr. Livingstone, that this is a fitting tribute to his memory, and we may remember the words of that distinguished traveller, who often spoke of that country as most healthy and suitable for such a settlement, " all will go right some " day, although I may not live to participate in the " joy, or even see the commencement of better times."

The Telegraph will be one of the most important agents in giving an impetus to enterprise, both moral and material. Hence the satisfaction with which we must regard the energetic efforts of the Cape Government and the Governments of Natal and the Orange Free State, in the establishment of a more complete system of land telegraph lines. And if this intercommunication in that country is advantageous, and to be encouraged, what arguments do I require to enforce what has already been urged by me before the Royal United Service Institution, that is to say, the duty of the Government of this country, both on Imperial and Colonial grounds, to lay, without loss of time, a Telegraphic Cable between England and the Cape Colony; for the great benefits to be derived from communication by telegraph in Africa will lose half their value, unless the Colony is linked with the mother country by an equally rapid means of intercourse ?

It may be taken as a matter of course that proper Roads in the Colonies must be made. This is the question for the East of Africa, and is now occupying the attention of those who are interested in the means of securing intercourse with the great interior lakes. To the farmer, the wool grower, the trader, to all, indeed, who live hundreds of miles to the north of the Cape and Natal, it is a matter of pressing necessity that there should be established the least difficult means of reaching the sea coast. Following the formation of suitable roads there is, naturally, the greater development of land carriage by the establish· ment of Railways. Nothing demonstrates more clearly the prosperity of the Cape, and its enterprise too, than the course which has been adopted by the

Cape Government and Parliament in their decision
to expend five millions sterling in the construction of railways.

Another great want of South Africa is suitable
Seaports and Harbours; for, excepting Cape Town,
there is no harbour where a vessel can lie in shelter,
and have the facilities which are required for loading
and discharging. Mossel Bay, Port Elizabeth
(Algoa Bay), Port Alfred, and East London, are all
open roadsteads; and at Durban, in Natal, it is
difficult to be certain of more than ten feet of water
on the bar. Sir John Coode, the eminent civil
engineer, has lately visited that country on the
invitation of the Cape Government, and has surveyed
all the ports. It will be extremely interesting
to hear what opinions he has formed as to the best
means to be adopted for securing greater facilities
to shipping at the seaports which I have named.

Then there are the elements of material
prosperity. The Gold Mine has played a remarkable part in the history of the world. It seems as
if Providence employed the attraction of gold to
draw men to people distant and neglected portions of
the globe. Hence the prosperity of California, the
advance of Australia, and the probable advance
of South Africa. But besides Gold, a bountiful
Nature has set throughout South Africa large mineral
wealth—cobalt, iron, silver, copper, manganese,
tin, lead, coal, not to speak of diamonds.

And as regards the soil and climate,* fruit and
grain of every description grow and flourish, wheat
as fine as that of California, the produce of the
tropics alongside of the fruits and productions with
which we are familiar in this country, and with an
abundance unknown to us. The fruitfulness of that
country, remarked by all travellers, requires only the
presence and energy of enterprising white men to
bring out its hidden illimitable resources.

Irrigation is one means which must have greater
attention in that country. One may wonder
that the bountiful showers which fall in Southern
Africa are not collected and stored for the
irrigation of the soil, and the use of the flocks and
herds of the inhabitants. I assume that all this will
follow a larger immigration, and the increase of
enterprise and wealth.

Immigration is one of the greatest wants of South
Africa; it must be encouraged by the Governments of
that country, following the example of Canada,
Australia, and New Zealand. One good result to
be expected from a union of the communities
of South Africa will be the harmonious arrangement of a general system of immigration.

---

* NOTE.—The climate of South Africa is very favourable to
persons of delicate constitution. There has recently been a marked
increase in the number of visitors to South Africa in search of health,
as well as for pleasure; and steps should be taken without delay to
provide suitable Hotel accommodation in the interior, and to
improve the facilities for travel.—*D.C.*

The Cape Colony has most worthily made
efforts to supply this want for itself. I remember President Burgers said to me there was
no use in the Transvaal spending money for
the introduction of immigrants, so long as the
Cape Government thought fit to import them at the
expense of the Colony, for that they found
their way into the Transvaal. To this I replied
that in my opinion, this fact, if a fact, should not
influence the Cape Government to alter their plans,
seeing that even if the people went into the Transvaal
they would help to develope its resources, and to bring
revenue to the Cape Colony itself. One of the most
important objects of the South African authorities
must be arrangements for immigration, and to
this end much has been done already. The
public works of the Colony have been supplied with
workmen by the Cape Emigration Commissioners in
this country, Messrs. Glanville and Burnet, whose
able and untiring exertions are devoted to obtaining
the very best class of men for the Colony. I
know that they are also most zealous and
successful in searching for and facilitating the trans-
port of those free emigrants who proceed to, or are
engaged for, South Africa. But I venture to urge, as I
have done officially in a communication to the Cape,
the vast advantage which will accrue to the Colony
if the Government can agree upon a thorough system,
such as has prevailed in Australia and New Zealand,

for the introduction of agriculturalists, masons,
joiners, carpenters, smiths, shepherds, and others;
men with a little money, or with what is as good,
suitable knowledge and handiness in their trades.
It is what New Zealand has accomplished successfully,
and even the Hawaian Government aims at a like result.
And this idea has had a start, for last week the Cape
Commissioners despatched in the steamer "Courland"
79 emigrants from Scotland, who have received the
promise of land in the Transkei upon an agreement
for its possession by them, they paying one shilling
per acre per month for 10 years, at the end of which
time the valuable land so granted to them is to be their
own property. The extension of this plan will be of the
utmost possible benefit to the Cape Colony; but it has
a limit, I fear, in this difficulty—that in South Africa
a large portion of the fertile lands has been allowed
to fall into the hands of speculators or others out
of the control of the Governments, so that there is not
the same power to give grants of land as in Australia
and in New Zealand. Nevertheless, it is quite plain
that due encouragement should be given in this
direction by the Colonial Governments; and no
greater benefit can accrue for the future development
of South Africa than from a well organized practical
system of free or assisted immigration.

The geographical position of the Cape Colony, as
commanding the Western route to India and Australia,
claims from the Imperial Government greater atten-

tion than it has received from a military and naval point of view: for with all the loyalty and courage of the people of South Africa, what humiliation would it bring if, through the neglect of the Home authorities, the harbours and coast were to suffer from the attacks of an enemy! This is not the place in which to enlarge upon the importance of Simon's Bay as a naval station, and the urgent necessity for the establishment of a Graving Dock there for the repair of the vessels of the British fleet: it will suffice if I simply indicate in this paper the readiness which I feel assured prevails throughout the English possessions in that quarter to join in any system of patriotic action with the mother country for colonial defence. One very interesting indication of the impulses of the people of South Africa in this direction may be found in the intention of some of the volunteers of the Cape Colony to visit this country, to compete with their brethren from Canada and Australia for the prizes offered at Wimbledon.

The Native Question is a great difficulty. And here I would venture to pay a tribute to the enlightened policy of the Cape Government towards the coloured races. The gradual extermination of the native population, as in America and in Australia, is not to be expected in South Africa. The Kafirs are there; they are capable of improvement; and it is our duty to treat them fairly, for they may be trained in time into useful members of the great

South African community.

The great destiny for South Africa I hold to be the overcoming of ignorance and the conquest of material oppositions throughout. In this I include an object dear to Englishmen, the gradual abolition of slavery, and in its place the establishment of commercial and agricultural advantages. Africa has been shut up for many centuries. It is to be opened up and receive within its borders, torn by war and oppressed by cruelty, the blessings of our civilization. This is not to be gained by wishing, or theorising, or by the presence of British Fleets on the Eastern or Western Coasts. Practical persistent common-sense efforts must be employed, in order that the whole country may be opened up. The merchants and traders will take their course northwards, the Boers in advance; trading stations will be established; farms opened out; mineral resources will be developed. Along the coast, the ports now under Portuguese authority will be occupied by agencies of the merchants of the southern ports; and due West into the interior, routes from the coast ports will open up communica-tions with the advancing communities inland. At present the Eastern Coast Ports do not facilitate intercourse with the interior, for the Portuguese are un-able to exercise control beyond their forts or stations near the coast. It is only necessary to refer to the reports of the British Consular Agents to discover the lament-

able state of matters on the Eastern Coast of Africa.[*]
It has been observed with striking comments
upon the prospects of the future of that part of the
world by the Consular Agents, that produce for
export, such as Coffee, which grows in perfection in
many parts of Africa, but which cannot pay for its
carriage *viâ* the Nile, might be enormously developed
if proper routes were made to the sea coast. And the
Consul at Zanzibar, in 1873, made this remark :
" If the difficult problem of the civilization of the
" wild tribes of inner Africa be surmountable, it will
" be by opening up facilities for commerce
" that it will be solved; for in the absence of
" such inducements, the, to them, distasteful work
" of cultivation will never progress beyond the
" servile labours of their women, which for ages have
" sufficed to supply their wants."

The Government of this country, by the establishment of a line of steamers between the Cape and
Zanzibar, and between Zanzibar and Aden, intended
to stimulate commercial intercourse, and thereby
assist in the abolition of the Slave Trade. It
is quite true that the Sultan of Zanzibar has fallen
in with the wishes of the Government by concluding
a treaty, but it has only had the effect of driving the

---

[*] NOTE.—The benevolent and enlightened efforts of His Majesty the King of the Belgians to give a new impulse to African exploration, with a view to the amelioration of the condition of the native races and the general development of the country, are now to have a practical result in the direction indicated. The Royal Geographical Society have also resolved to take steps for opening out Routes into Central Africa, from the Eastern and South Eastern Coast.—*D.C.*

slave trade to pass by land northwards, with additional
sufferings to the captives. Indeed, in the coast ports
there is the same need for supervision and vigilance as
before. I am satisfied that the proper course
for the Government to take is to encourage steamships
trading along the coast to make such places as
Mozambique and the mouths of the Zambesi ports of
destination, or of longer call for the steamers than at
present, in order that a permanent influence may
be exerted upon the people. But beyond this, I may
say that it is not reasonable to expect that there
can be any diminution in the traffic in slaves, or
any advancement in the desire for freedom to them,
so long as we fail to recognise the fact that the
slave trade is encouraged by many Indian Banians
as well as by Arab traders. It is not through
the connection with India and the Persian Gulf that
the slave trade is to be controlled, seeing that
there is a population in those parts providing a
market for the traffic, and an asylum for such
as have made their fortunes by the trade. In
my judgment South Africa, with its British
people and enterprise, is the country which is
to have the honor of abolishing slavery, by the
encouragement of industry.

Legitimate trade on the East Coast has shown
a marked increase since the establishment of steam
navigation. In the report of Captain Prideaux,
Her Majesty's Consul at Zanzibar, with respect

to trade and commerce for the years 1873-4, immediately after mail steamers had been placed upon the line between Aden, Zanzibar, and the Cape, there appears a striking comparison between the course of trade before and after the establishment of a steam service and the new regulations of the Sultan of Zanzibar for the suppression of the slave trade on the coast. Partly owing to the difficulty of finding out from those who farm the Customs in the Zanzibar territory, and partly from the objection of the limited number of merchants who have mercantile houses at the sea board, and who are naturally jealous of rivalry, it has always been difficult to obtain the exact data which indicate the progress of commerce in imports and exports. The Slave Trade, however, evidently still continues. The importation of arms, beads, and wire, which shewed a marked decrease in 1872-3, somewhat recovered its position in 1873-4, and for this reason:—the negociations for the treaty of 1873 gave ground for uneasiness to the merchants who supply the slave dealers, and while negociations were in progress, a virtual stop was put to the trade. In 1873-4 the trade was renewed, and the Consul properly mentions this as " a melancholy proof of the vitality of the land traffic " to which the public attention is now directed."

The efforts which England has made for the suppression of the slave trade on the East Coast of South Africa and in the Mozambique Channel, and the exertions of our Consuls and Naval Officers merit the highest praise. The naval officers have very little assistance, official reports state, from any other power. Consul Elton, in his last report, has stated that the Portuguese made no exertions at sea to hinder the traffic, except, indeed, one or two short trips of a little steamer, which for the rest of the year sheltered itself in Mozambique. In May 1875, Rear-Admiral Cumming wrote to the Secretary of the Admiralty as follows:—" That slavery exists, and to a great " extent, in Mozambique is unquestioned : but before " the navy can put a stop to this they must have " greater powers. The navy know full well that " their present work is all in vain." And here I may mention one hindrance to the development of traffic along the coast, namely, that the coasting trade could only be carried on under the Portuguese flag, except in the case of mail steamers.

The development of the trade of the coast ports situated between Zanzibar and Natal will hereafter be best secured through river carriage by the natural channels, such as the Zambesi. The improved caravan roads which have been suggested will naturally offer the points of junction for the traders and immigrants from the Cape Colony on their civilising march to the north; but as the whole line of coast between Delagoa Bay and Zanzibar is in the hands of the Portu- guese Government, the question may be asked what will Portugal do to assist us ? The honor of discovery, and the right of conquest and possession, gave to the Portuguese this length of sea board, a narrow strip of land, within whose limits their authority is not always respected or recognised, and beyond whose borders very little traffic from the east enters and spreads itself. The English Consul at Mozambique, in his report for 1875, referring to this large extent of sea coast possessions, which he estimates at 1200 miles in extent, says that " the furthest points " in the interior occupied by the Portuguese are on " the Zambesi river, where a few men were recently " stationed as high as Zumba, but are now withdrawn " to Tete." He states distinctly, that " there are no " posts held in the interior by the Portuguese on the " East Coast of Africa elsewhere than in their district " of Zambezia." The whole of this territory is capable of great development, but how can this be furthered by Portuguese influence, if, according to Consul Elton's report, " the finances of Mozambique are in " a deplorable state, and naturally affect trade? " Money has been borrowed from the French mer- " chants to meet the military pay, and every penny " is sent to the capital to keep the machinery of the " Local Government from coming to a sudden stand- " still." Under such circumstances it may become a matter for serious consideration whether any power is justified in impeding commerce and civilization by the exercise of a merely nominal sovereignty.

The future prospects of South Eastern Africa

depend in a large measure upon the use which the
Government of Portugal may make of the port of
Lorenço Marques, or Delagoa Bay. Situated in
close proximity to the Transvaal and the Zulu
Kingdom, it offers to these districts, as well as
to the whole of the Portuguese possessions to the
north, and to the interior up to the Zambezi, a source
of supply and means of export quite unique. There
is an unlimited depth of water for shipping : the
harbour is safe, and the trade with Mozambique and
the East African Coast ports could be largely increased.
There is to be a railway between the Bay and the
borders of the Transvaal. The question arises then,
will Portugal press forward its development, not merely
establishing there a military station, but making it a
centre of influence and of commercial life ? Delagoa
Bay has offered hitherto most dangerous facilities to
the Kafirs for the purchase of gunpowder, cheap
guns, and spirits. It is not an uncommon thing for
hundreds of Zulus to be seen at and near Delagoa Bay,
waiting for a delivery of guns, and under a treaty
made with President Burgers this facility was to be
increased by a reduction of the duty. This implies
a grave danger, aggravated by the utter absence of
control, as Consul Elton states, by the Portuguese
beyond their own port.

The Government of Portugal, as may be seen
from their communications with our Government,
are now deeply interested in carrying out every

practicable measure in their power for the development and prosperity of the territories under their control on the East Coast of Africa. I am quite aware that our Blue Books show great laxity on the part of the officials of Portugal in Africa. It is to be regretted that that Government has not hitherto been able to establish such Agencies by liberal payment and with suitable assistance as are required ; but it is to be hoped that the enlightened purpose of the Government of Lisbon to encourage trade, and to abolish the slave traffic in harmony with England, will impress upon them the necessity for a liberal and extended expenditure and supervision. The Government is not altogether to blame : we must look to the limited means which circumstances have allowed them to employ in the prosecution of a task so onerous and responsible as the supervision and control of a sea coast of 1,200 miles in extent.

In Natal the sale of guns is placed under restrictions for the very purpose of preventing any supply of arms to the native tribes; but Consul Elton, the British representative at Mozambique, makes this remark in his report :—
" All our precautions and legislations are nullified
" by the existence of an armoury on our flank," and he adds, " this opens a question of the gravest
" consequences, and demands serious consideration."
Another danger and injury to the people and to

the future of the country exists in the unregulated
sale of spirits to such tribes as the Amatongas,
a system which it has been officially reported
" is fast demoralising the country." I have not
invented these reflections, but have drawn the
information mentioned from official sources. For
my own part, I express the conviction that the
enlightened humanity of the Portuguese Government
will dictate to the authorities of Lorenço Marques
such regulations as will secure freedom from a danger
threatening to them and to England, and to the
maintenance of amicable relations between their
Governments. For it should be remembered that not
a century ago Kafirs surrounded the town of
Lorenço Marques, dismantled the fortress, seized
the Governor, Ribeiro, and murdered him bar-
barously. The present time offers a fine opportunity for the extension of a plan of Confederation
to Lorenço Marques itself, and, if the Portuguese
would have it, as far north as, or further than,
Mozambique. Joint action between Portugal and
England in the native question, the supply of arms,
the sale of spirits, the suppression of the slave trade,
and all that is included in progress and civilization,
would offer not merely a grand spectacle of harmonious action for the races placed within our
influence, but would secure such an increase of wealth
as would amply repay all the trouble and expense
incurred; and the transfer to the British Crown

of the Transvaal territory affords an opportunity for the immediate consideration of these important questions.

Upon this theory of development inland from the East, through Portuguese territory, as compared with influences from the South, through the energy of men of the English race, I will give the following words from one of our Government reports :—" On " the Zambezi water communication exists, but " nowhere else do the Portuguese attempt, as a rule, " to penetrate the interior of Africa, neither do they " avail themselves of the Angoxa, Moma, Kisungo, " Busi, Sabia, Limpopo, King Georges', or the Maputa " rivers, all means of communication, for the extension " of trade and the civilization of the country; but, on " the contrary, they do their very best to keep those " rivers hermetically closed to lawful trade, in order " to avoid prejudice to the Custom Houses they have " established at a few scattered points, held upon the " seaboard of the coast, over which they claim an " entire sovereignty, but in reality exercise no juris- " diction, save over the fortified ' comptoirs ' and on " the Zambezi : as a result, in the district of " Mozambique the slave trade is carried on from " most of the rivers fronting Madagascar, because " the returns are enormous, and one cargo run " out of three or four gives a large profit, for the " would-be legal trader, who cannot afford to lose " one venture out of twenty, is driven by the circum-

" locution and operation of Customs' regulations he
" fails to understand into the slave trade in the hope
" of rapid gains, knowing that if denounced at
" Mozambique as doing 'a contraband lawful trade,'
" an opportunity will be watched for to seize and
" confiscate his dhow."

This future of Southern and Eastern Central
Africa, to extend to the distant West, as well as to the
North, is to be developed on principles which have
an interest to us all in England itself, as concerned
in the whole Colonial Empire. For I may remind you
of the words the noble Earl the Secretary of State for
the Colonies employed lately in the House of Lords.
They have in them a prophecy as well as a conviction, quite in accord with the feelings of the members
of this Institute, indicating a future, distant it may
be, but still a future nearer than men care to
believe. Lord Carnarvon said :-- " Nor can I
" see any reason why in the nature of things, and
" apart from those fugitive causes which do not belong
" to the fixed and unchanging principles of political
" life, the dependencies of the British Crown should
" any more than any other States be incapable of
" Confederation. It is quite possible that Confeder-
" ation is only one stage in the political journey of
" the Empire, and that it may even lead in the
" course of time to a still closer union. But, be this
" as it may, the reason why I now urge this measure
" for the adoption of Parliament, is that such a

" principle of Confederation must add strength to
" these colonies, give larger objects, a higher policy, a
" wider political life, and, as I earnestly hope, a better
" security for the right treatment of the native races.
" And if so, all this means greater prosperity and
" peace—a closer cosolidation of imperial interests.
" The English Empire is, no doubt, vast, various, and
" disconnected ; and yet when all allowance and
" deduction have been made, it is, I am prepared to
" maintain, one of the most wonderful pieces of human
" administration the world has ever seen, both in
" what it does and what it does not do. Other
" countries have founded Colonial Empires. France,
" Spain. and Portugal have left their mark on the
" colonial history of the world, and yet as colonising
" powers they have virtually ceased to exist; and,
" among other reasons, for this, that they were
" founded upon a close principle of restriction. We
" have adopted a different system ; we have discarded
" restrictions ; we have looked to freedom of Govern-
" ment as our ultimate object, and we have been
" rewarded by an almost immeasurable freedom of
" growth."

I shall trespass no longer upon the time which
remains for discussion; others better acquainted with
the details will offer you more light upon the matters
to which I have referred. It is enough for me
that I have been allowed to draw attention to
some considerations which apply to the present

and future condition of South Africa, a country
in which I take a deep interest, and whose welfare
and prosperity have been the object of continued
concern to the members of the Royal Colonial
Institute.

THE FOLLOWING IS A REPORT OF THE DISCUSSION
WHICH APPEARED IN "THE COLONIES AND INDIA"
OF 23rd JUNE, 1877.

Mr. FROUDE said he had attended there that evening not expect-
ing to be called upon to say anything, but to listen to Mr. Donald
Currie. It was difficult to limit what could be said to the customary
ten minutes; and as to what he might wish to say, as it was on South
Africa he felt a little shy in speaking on the subject. As he was present,
it was but natural that they would expect him to say something
about his own short connection with that country; but there were
difficulties to be encountered in going into the matter on account of
the many sensitive points involved on which it was undesirable to
touch. Perhaps, however, they would allow him the opportunity of
stating what passed between himself and Mr. Molteno when Mr.
Molteno was in England last year. On his (Mr. Froude's) first visit
to the Cape, Mr. Molteno was exceedingly kind to him—indeed,
much more than kind—and afforded him every opportunity of seeing
and hearing everything to be seen and heard, besides giving him the
benefit of his (Mr. Molteno's) large knowledge of the Colony. He
(Mr. Froude) certainly thought he had understood Mr. Molteno.
But there had been points left imperfectly explained. When Mr.
Froude went out again to the Cape there was a certain degree
of misunderstanding which led to disagreements. When, however,
Mr. Molteno was in England last year, he and Mr. Froude came to
a thorough understanding that there had been mutual mistakes;
that neither had intended in the slightest degree to do anything of
which either had a right to complain; and therefore they agreed
not to go into any details. There he would now wish to leave the
matter, with the words which Mr. Molteno used in parting with him,
" All's well that ends well." He (Mr. Froude) was sure they must
all thank Mr. Donald Currie for the careful and elaborate analysis
he had given of the present state of South Africa. There was
hardly a point he had left untouched, and it all showed a marvellous
insight into the different races, the different interests, the large
resources in all directions which admitted of being opened out.
The different objects on which Mr. Currie had touched were so many
that he could not attempt to follow him through. He would
confine himself to one, on which Mr. Currie had entered with least
detail; he meant the native question. It derived importance from
the recent great acquisition of the Transvaal territory. The white
races in South Africa, he conceived, might have their little differ-
ences and difficulties in arriving at confederation or any other

arrangement of their affairs which they might like to make; but the white races in South Africa could be trusted to take care of themselves; and there might be a little pushing and shouldering before parties fell into their natural places, but this was a matter of slight and secondary consideration. We had had rather to think of that enormous mass of people who were now subordinated to us, and for whom, by taking over that country, we had now made ourselves responsible —he alluded to the Zulu and other native tribes in the Cape Colony, and in Natal, and in the Transvaal. He believed he was right in saying that, if all the natives were put together, it would be found that there were 400,000 in Natal, and about 800,000 more in the Cape Colony and its dependencies. There were nearly 200,000 in Basuto Land. In Kaffraria and in the Colony 500,000 or 600,000. In the Transvaal, by a stroke of Sir Theophilus Shepstone's pen, there had just been added about a million more; and all round the Transvaal there were vast powerful native tribes, numbering it was difficult to say how many—there were probably a million and a half with whom we should be brought into immediate relations in consequence of the annexation. Those people we should not allow to make war any more, and thus keep their numbers from increasing. They were extremely prolific, and he asked what would they be at the end of fifty years? There would be six or seven millions of them at least; and there lay a serious responsibility in us to discover by what means those people could be reclaimed from their present savagery and elevated into civilised communities. It would occupy a long time and was extremely intricate. They were not to be recovered in a few years, but by a series of laborious efforts, which would tax all the energies of the Imperial Government and the colonists alike. The nations of Europe had taken thousands of years to reach their present state; and it was not to be supposed that by simply making the black races free, by giving them equal rights, and teaching them the multiplication tables, that a change could be effected at once, which would put them on a level with the white races. It could not be done. Left to a mere collision of interests, they would go to the wall. There would be an inferior race and a superior race simply contending one against the other for the same objects, with what was called equal rights. He knew well what would become of all that. The weaker party would fall. Therefore there lay before us—whether under a system of Confederation or whatever it might be—one of the hardest problems, in the solution of which England must bear her share. It was their first duty. Beyond all questions of diamonds, gold diggings, and ostrich breeding, this first duty was staring us in the face, what were to be our future relations with the native races in South Africa. Elsewhere those relations proved one of the saddest chapters in British history. One after another the inferior races with whom we had come in contact had died out before us. In the Zulus we have to deal with a noble, excellent people, a people that must not be allowed to perish, as the American Indians or the savages of Australia or New Zealand. In honour and conscience we must make an effort to preserve the Zulus. In some way or other the Zulu people would have to be dealt with; and he earnestly hoped that English people at home and in South Africa would recognize their obligation and try to fulfil it. In doing that duty the colonists would themselves receive a higher moral training; they would themselves become a greater people in endeavouring to accomplish a difficult work in an honourable way than if they had piled together the largest fortunes that were ever made in a British province, or could show more diamonds than ever grew in the garden of Aladdin.

Sir JOHN COODE did not expect to be called upon to say anything; he would, however, on the spur of the moment offer a few remarks. Mr. Donald Currie had been good enough to refer to his (Sir John Coode's) recent visit to South Africa in order to examine the coasts for the Governments of the Cape Colony, and of Natal. That he had done, and he hoped it would not be expected that he should enlarge upon that subject, because he must not now anticipate what he should have to say in official documents. He would only make a remark or two on some of the points which had fallen from Mr. Currie in the course of his paper—a remarkable paper, when it was remembered that the author had never visited that country. The two subjects which most attracted his attention as the most pressing wants of the Colony, were those of immigration and irrigation. The greatest of all wants of South Africa now was labour. That, he thought, no one who had visited the colony for only a short period could doubt for a moment. He referred with satisfaction to the fact that the Cape Government were beginning to realise the importance of immigration. He was happy to think that that was so, and that at the port of East London—which was now in immediate connection, by railway, with an important and productive part of the Colony in the neighbourhood of King William's Town—the Government had erected a barrack, which was just finished at the time of his visit, the object of which barrack was to accommodate in its present state fifty Scotch families. The Government had arranged that those emigrants that went out in parties of fifty families at a time were in the first instance to be passed on into the interior; this was the commencement of what he hoped would eventually prove to be one of the greatest steps in the way of supplying labour for the cultivation of the soil in South Africa. As regarded irrigation, that, perhaps, was the next most important point imperially. During the last few years they had suffered very little from drought. Time was not very long ago when there was very great suffering in the Colony arising from successive dry seasons. But even in what was considered an ordinary season in South Africa there was a great lack of water at certain times of the year, and the total annual rainfall was, as a rule, not insufficient by any means. But inasmuch as those rains usually only fell during a very few months in the year, there was great necessity for the construction of works for the storage of water, in order that it might contribute to the fertilisation of lands, and the production of crops, during the dry parts of the year. The Dutch themselves had done a great deal in that direction. He was sorry he had not been able to visit that district, which lay to the north of

George Town, about the central part of South Coast. There was a district there called Oudtshoorn, where the Dutch had some most remarkable examples of what that country might be made to produce by proper irrigation. The Cape Government, not above two years since, engaged Mr. Gamble, C.E., to take up the Department of Irrigation. This gentleman had been engaged in the Colony, and had made several reports; but as a matter of fact very little had, he believed, been as yet done. Government's attention had been directed to it, and he hoped they would be induced to promote in every way the construction of dams there to impound the water for the benefit of the Colony. Those were, perhaps, two of the most important questions affecting the Cape Colony at the present time. With regard to the introduction of arms, he was afraid that upon that point he should be obliged to differ from Mr. Donald Currie, for the mischief was to a great extent pretty well done. As respected Zulu Land he had it from the highest authority that not only were the men well supplied with arms, but the women also, and the women practised, and were most expert in their use. Whether that was for the sake of sport, or whether it be with a view to future mischief, he was unable to say, not having been able to obtain any satisfactory information on that point. But there remained the fact, and his authority, if he were to name it, would make it unquestionable, that both the men and women in Zulu Land did practise with firearms. Now in Kaffraria it was different. The ordinary Kafir was a very thrifty individual; they had a great passion for the possession of fire-arms, but did not care to expend money in the purchase of ammunition. He did not know that he had anything more to say with regard to the other matters touched upon in Mr. Currie's able paper. His attention during the time he was in the Colony was, he might say, entirely directed to the particular object for which he went out. But those points as to the necessity for emigration on a large scale, and the need for irrigation works, he could not dwell upon too strongly. He could foresee with a large emigration a marvellous future development of the productive power of the Colony, if only the Government would introduce agricultural labour on a comprehensive scale, encourage that labour, and promote in some way, by loans or otherwise, the formation of dams, in order that the country might have the fullest possible benefit of the rains which fell from the heavens. (Cheers.)

Colonel CROSSMAN also expressed himself as not having expected to be called upon to address the meeting; but as they had asked him to say some words upon the subject he should be glad to do so. The only part of Cape Colony that he knew anything about was—that just now about to be attached to it—Griqualand West. The diamond fields there were sources of great wealth to the Colony, a very great source of wealth indeed, and they had been the means of introducing into the Colony a large number of people, who had tended to the advancement of the country. He was glad that province was to be added to the Cape Colony, and he hoped, now that the Transvaal difficulty had been removed, that the whole of the other provinces, with the Orange Free State, would in a short time form part of a great South African Confederation, though no doubt the citizens of the Orange Free State were very happy as they were at present. He was in great hopes that before long that State would come into the Confederation, as he trusted all the provinces in South Africa would. For advancement in the future of Cape Colony they must have railways, harbours, and telegraphs. He thought they were doing all they could at present; at least, whatever difference there might be in opinion as regarded the direction in which the railways should be carried, there was no doubt that the Cape Government had before it the necessity of constructing railways all through the Colony; and whether they went through the Colony by Beaufort West or by any other route up to Griqualand West, and so on to the Transvaal, he thought it was one of the first things that ought to be done. As regarded harbours, Sir John Coode had been out there lately, and had gone into the question very carefully, and he must say that schemes for the improvement of Table Bay, Port Elizabeth, and the other harbours would be well worked out by so distinguished an engineer. As regarded also the question of irrigation, Mr. Gamble had gone out there lately, and he hoped the country would benefit by his reports. If the Cape Colony went on making railways, improving their harbours, carrying out irrigation works, &c., he was sure that, whatever expense might be incurred in doing so, it would be repaid hereafter. As regards other matters connected with the advancement of the Colony, it was not for him to say anything about affairs which were for the consideration of the Colonists themselves. Mr. Froude had been to the Cape, and had done more probably than anyone else to teach the people how beneficial it would be for them to enter into some confederation scheme. He hoped there would be no jealousy between rival provinces as to which place should be chosen as the capital. Cape Town, no doubt the most important place at the present moment in the Cape Colony, looked forward to being so, but other growing provinces put in their claims. He might venture to suggest that as in Canada they fixed upon a small town upon the river Ottawa as the capital of the Dominion, and as in the United States they took Washington as the chief place of the Republic, that the Cape Colonies might take into consideration whether it would not be advisable to choose some place in the interior fairly accessible to all, and so perhaps prevent any jealousies which would be sure to arise if a larger place were selected. He concluded by remarking that he took a deep interest in the Cape Colony and South Africa generally, and he was sure that that portion of the British Empire was advancing and would advance as rapidly as any other part of her Majesty's dominions.

Mr. HOUSTON remarked that he was going to draw attention to what had been rather taken out of his mouth by Mr. Froude, for he always thought "the native question" was the most important for South Africa. Many people seemed to have an idea that South Africa could be made out of its various States, like Australia, New Zealand, or

Canada. Now it seemed to him that that was entirely wrong. In all those Colonies the natives had been very few in number to begin with, and they had all died out. They had had the Anglo-Saxon race and all the resources requisite for colonising developed. But in South Africa, as pointed out by Mr. Froude, in the course of fifty years the black population would be three or four times as numerous as it was to-day. They were now numerous enough, and if we civilized them as one race, as was intended should be done, they must have land; and if the Kafirs and all the black people had territory—for land was not unavailable for the white man, therefore, he considered—especially since the annexation of the Transvaal—the native question and the land question became intermixed. The only point remained was, what population was it desirable to introduce? He was inclined to think that capitalists should be first secured, followed by an influx of the artisan class. As they pretended to be a colonising race, our object ought to be to civilise and make use of the black population for the small shopkeeper, artisans, grooms, servants, and everything else out of the black population. (Hear, hear.) Therefore it appeared to him that there was no very great field, except in the immediate future, for European immigration into South Africa. As Mr. Froude pointed out, the question of the native race remained, with regard to civilising and making them perform the ordinary duties of life. The only other point to which he would allude was that people in this country seemed rather too much to talk about Colonies and the Cape. Now, from Cape Town into the Transvaal was 1,400 miles as the crow flies, and everything in the Transvaal was very different from what was found in the Cape. There was so much time wasted in talking about South Africa that he rather despaired of a solution being found; he rather despaired of the different questions concerning South Africa being settled until Confederation was brought about, there were so many questions that could only be settled by a Union Parliament. At present each Colony and each different race had different ways; and thus the Anglo-Saxon race was split up in South Africa into sections. Each section looked at these questions from its own point of view. Therefore he thought that Confederation alone would settle those questions—to many of which allusion had been made that night. It became therefore very important that, instead of trying to settle those questions ourselves here, we should rather do all we could to forward Confederation, hoping that the Union Parliament would be strong enough—as he believed it would be—to settle their own affairs, including, also, the native affairs. Having been called upon unexpectedly to speak, those were about all the remarks he had to make. (Loud cheers.)

The Hon. EVELYN ASHLEY, M.P., said that without affectation it was an unexpected honour conferred on him to be called upon to speak. But as he believed he was the only member of the House of Commons present, it would not be out of place if he rose to thank Mr. Donald Currie for his interesting lecture that evening. It was a very useful address on a pressing question for the legislature of the present day. Although our legislators were always anxious to do the best they could for the aid and prosperity of the Colonies, still he confessed that in a popular assembly like the House of Commons there was very great ignorance on many Colonial matters (hear, hear); especially in a case of this sort—which was not a simple question. Anybody who had heard the discussion that night would see that there were embraced in the question of South African confederation not only the jealousies of governing races, not only the disabilities of inferior races, not only what might be called the springs of free government and of material prosperity in the Colonies, but, above all, what were the urgent responsibilities which the Imperial Government must be called upon to undertake in helping to settle the question. Therefore a discussion like this was most useful in spreading information. Within the narrow limit of time allowed, and the equally narrow limits of his knowledge on this subject, it would be wrong to enter into it at any length. But he would say that he felt deeply convinced that the speakers that evening had touched upon the great difficulty we had before us—that was, the treatment of the native races. (Hear, hear.) What must be done when this question —as far as the discussion of it in the House of Commons was concerned—was to guard against running into either of the two dangerous extremes. We must avoid one extreme—namely, saying : " Throw open the whole basis of Government, and give the Kafir and other tribes the franchise right and left." (Hear, hear.) Nobody could be more anxious than he to raise and improve the natives all the world over. But nobody could view that question without seeing that not only would a bad feeling be created between us and the Colony if such an extreme course were pursued, but great harm would also arise to the natives themselves. At the same time they must earnestly repudiate the other extreme, and never say that colour alone is to be a mark of disability. That would be contrary to our wishes and our duty, and would place a bar to the raising of the natives which Mr Froude and the last speaker had referred to as the objects we had to undertake. (Hear, hear.) To guide our course wisely and moderately between those two extremes must be the object of her Majesty's loyal subjects on both continents. Now as to the difficulty of bringing those different States to unite in Confederation. It struck him, although with his limited knowledge he might be wrong, that one of the great difficulties must be the individual jealousies of newly established communities, and the great dread of the leading men in each State of losing their position, so recently gained and so likely to be swamped by being submerged in a larger community. (Hear, hear.) If that was the case, he thought they might congratulate themselves that we had sent out to the Cape to superintend, if our hopes are realised, the formation of that Confederation, a man who united to highest tact the highest character for judgment—he alluded to Sir Bartle Frere. They might be sure that they could not have had a more admirably adapted man to carry out the objects for which he was sent, for he in an eminent degree combined with the largest views of an administrator that great sympathy for the native races which he (Mr. Ashley) declared must be the guiding star of our course. (Great cheers.)

Mr. ANTHONY TROLLOPE said if they had postponed the discussion of this question for nine months, he might then, perhaps, be better able to address them than he now was; for it was his fate to be going to entrust himself to the tender mercies of Mr. Donald Currie in the course of this month, whose ship he hoped would carry him safely to Cape Town, from which place it was his intention to endeavour to see something of those subjects which were before them, and to return home and in a humble way describe, not with his voice—for he was not much given to speaking—but with his pen (cheers), to tell them something which he only trusted would not be taken altogether for fiction. He had been happy to hear Mr. Donald Currie tell them they would find the annexation of the districts of South Africa—with that great question of which Mr. Ashley and the House of Commons were discussing the previous night—was carried out so satisfactorily ; and if he could bring home the information from there he might be able to fill our regiments with recruits —at any rate, he would endeavour to see the country and form a fair judgment of it. As he intended to appear to go out with his mind blank, he should not express any opinion at all. If he had an opinion on the subject of annexation—if he had an opinion as to the merits or demerits of Sir Theophilus Shepstone—he should keep it to himself, so that when he came home, at the expiration perhaps of nine months, he might be able to ascertain and point out all about it without any preconceived ideas at all. He thought he might say, without pretending to have made up his mind on any vexed point, that with regard to the annexation of that country, whoever may have been wrong, whoever may have been unfortunate—whether England may have been unfortunate in having it annexed, whether Lord Carnarvon may have been unfortunate in authorising as far as he did annexation, whether Sir Theophilus Shepstone was unfortunate in annexing it, or whether the English or other Colonists there had been unfortunate, he thought they all felt that for the multitude for which Mr. Froude had so eloquently pleaded the annexation must be fortunate. (Hear, hear.) He had visited all the large English-speaking countries now except that one, and no doubt the difficulty with regard to all those countries which had struck us with horror had been the fact that, in carrying out our instincts for civilising and utilising the countries which God had given us, we had never, with all our efforts and good intentions, been able to treat the natives in a manner which was wholly satisfactory. (Hear, hear.) Efforts were made on the grandest principles of philanthropy in New Zealand. When we first took New Zealand as our own we annihilated contracts which had been made by English men and by English communities, in order that the natives might there stand on their own soil, and be able to say—and in order that we might be able to say also—that they had been robbed of nothing and that we had deprived them of nothing. But we knew how terrible had been the fate of those natives. As Mr. Froude had said, they were dying out. In Australia they had died out ; in Tasmania utterly, there was not one left. In Australia they were dying out so fast that in the most populous parts of the

country there was hardly one. We knew what had been the fate
of the unfortunate Indians over the territory which we own, and of
which the most populous part was held by our greatest Colonists—
the citizens of the United States. They were going, or had gone.
But there was a race which we hope, and which every man in that
room hoped—a race that need not go. (Hear, hear.) Now what
we have to look after was this, whether in annexing those countries
that race would not have a better chance of insuring and living in
prosperity and comfort, and enjoying the gifts of God—whether
it would not have a better chance by the annexation of the districts
than it would if they were left divided as they had been and now
were. (Hear, hear.) He did not intend to dwell on that subject,
and only mentioned it as a point which, of all others, would be
most interesting to him in the tour he was about to make. (Hear,
hear.)

Mrs. AMELIA LEWIS said the last time she ventured to address
the Royal Colonial Institute was on the occasion when Mr. Wilson
read his very remarkable paper about our taking a larger interest
and introducing into the Colonies those sustenances of which we make
our happiness most at home. She had for some years past enquired
into the whole causes of social combinations, and nothing had
impressed her more than the vast influence which Colonial life must
bring back again upon the home country—the home country going
out with its influences on the new races, and the latter bringing
sometimes one or the other to their new parents the influence back to
home. In a few words, she had to plead against the dreadful ignorance which was existing in the whole country on the whole of the
Colonial subjects. (Cheers.) She declared that the ignorance was
so great that a boy who could tell what the Sabines of the old
Roman were sent for, could not tell about the grand races of which
this little country, the small Anglo-Saxon race—excepting only the
Greeks—the only nation that had successfully colonised the globe.
(Hear, hear.) Why were not the people who came before our much-
beloved country known about? It would give us more chance to
know something than all the schools in the land taught. She
instanced Oxford and Cambridge as no exception to the rule. She
had had the pleasure of listening to an historical lecture at Oxford,
about which lectures she thought she knew something. She was
born of an old, venerable man who served as the first translator for
this country at the Foreign Office, the late Mr. Hutton, through whom
she had been introduced to knowledge from which she had benefited.
She declared that it was necessary this country should be awakened
to an appreciation of the education of the boys—and for that matter
girls—and make them acquainted with the bearings of Colonial life,
colonial history, and what the Colonies brought to us. (Hear, hear.)
Need she quote anything more than the beautiful words of Mr.
Burke when he stood before the House of Commons and pronounced
that remarkable speech of his on the reconciliation of North America,
and recommended them at the beginning of last Session. He said :—
" You exported 86,000 to Africa; at the end of about one hundred

years you had 866,000; what do you export now?" And as Mr. Fowler said, it was not a matter of exports only, it was also a matter of imports. There was wanted much that this country was neglecting—that is to say, cultivation, which was her study. (Hear, hear.) She had already sacrificed something for that, and she asserted that it was from the Colonies that they were to ask for much of the vigour which was got. (Hear, hear.) She declared that the subject which would have to be introduced was education, and she trusted the time would come when some great men would take up this question and would at once " cotton " to the way in which history was now taught in schools. We wanted living history. (Hear, hear.) Men and women that went out to those Colonies had to bear with a different climate from their own. Only a little while ago a father who had nurtured his daughter into the greatest nicety, sent a letter to the *Echo* newspaper to describe her retirement in South Africa, which no doubt had a large future. Her own ideas on South Africa were such that they were scarcely possible to be good enough and to recognise humbly the claims which that vast country demanded. Therefore she trusted her few words, if they only left an impression on a few of those men that had large influence, that the time had come when something should be done, and something that should emanate from that Society she was addressing, to make the working men and women and the public generally acquainted in a large sense, by which she meant emigration to Africa; they ought not to think that Africa meant, like a small paragraph in a daily newspaper would lead them to suppose, a place abounding with gorillas, but a glorious country. (Hear, hear.) It was she assured them a serious subject, and one upon which, traced to the highest and lowest society, the greatest ignorance prevailed. (Great cheering.)

Governor Rowe, C.M.G. (West African Settlements), said the subject of the treatment of the natives in South Africa was one of very considerable interest to him. Of the South African Colonies he had no personal knowledge; but he had of the natives of Equatorial Africa, based upon an experience of years. The future of Africa he believed depended upon the action of the races that had lived there for centuries. The people who were going to cultivate Africa he believed were the aboriginal inhabitants, the negro people—the Hottentots, the black people who had lived in Africa probably for a longer period than our race in England; and the fact that those races did not disappear before the white man, was a proof that some day they would cultivate Africa and would develope its very many products for our use. (Hear, hear.) He did not believe for one moment that we should have any insuperable difficulty in dealing with them. There were, and would be always, difficulties in carrying out anything that was worth carrying out; but he felt sure that unless our race had altered very much, or did alter very much—if the ruling principle of England was animated by the same feelings of justice towards the negro that it had always been, and by that same firmness as well as fairness which was characteristic of our nation, we should get over all the difficulties which presented themselves to us, and the result would be that the black people of Africa would not be a source of weakness to us but a source of strength. (Hear, hear.)

Mr. F. D. ARCHER (a native of Barbadoes) had listened to some very interesting speeches and an admirable paper on South Africa— a subject in which he must necessarily be interested, being of African descent—he thought he could not on behalf of the Colonies better approve the sentiments expressed than by saying a few words in acknowledgment of such kindly expressions of sympathy towards people of the African race. He could not say very much about South Africa, not having been there, but with regard to the matter of the annexation (of the Transvaal) he thought there could be no doubt that it was one of the grandest things that could have been performed by the British Government, as it would for ever settle the question of slavery there. In the Transvaal, slavery had existed in a somewhat disguised form for some time, and if now the British Government, who had put down slavery in their own Colonies, should take on themselves the duty of stopping it effectually in that quarter, that must, he thought, rather be regarded as a cause of triumphant congratulation to all interested in the welfare of the natives than otherwise. (Hear, hear.) He did not know what might be meant by Confederation from a political point of view; he did not pretend to understand much about it. If, however, it meant that all those States should be drawn together under one Government, and that that Government should be influenced by dictates of justice and humanity towards the people occupying those States, then he would say, let them have Confederation by all means. (Cheers.) That the civilised nations of the earth should, on going into other countries, and as civilised people, endeavour to depress the people of those countries, seemed to him altogether but the restoration of ideas of the state of barbarism which existed thousands of years ago. If they looked at the conduct of the Romans, who were the greatest conquerors earth had seen, it would be found that they tried to impress their civilisation on the nations they conquered; and so let England go forward—not to damp the energies of native races, but to aid them to rise to the standard of true men, to aid them to see that it was meant towards them and their kinsmen, that, equally as other men, they should enjoy the blessings of the earth, and be good and serviceable members of the communities to which they belonged. He knew well that there was always a conflict of the races. Whenever men of white complexions and men of black complexions met there ever seemed to be a bone of contention between them. The one, from his superior civilisation, looked down upon the other, and that man who through his ignorance could not compete with the more intellectual individual had to give way. But the individual who was blessed with the greater knowledge had a duty before him, which was that it should be his object to extend a helping hand to his fellow-man, to lift him up from his degraded position, in order that he might be even what the great God who made of one flesh and blood all the families of the earth intended him to be. He did not know what might be the future of South

Africa, but if he could trust to the humanity and justice which had ever been manifested by the British Government in their dealings with the Colonies, which in the providence of God had come under their power, he would say that there was a great future in store, not only for South Africa, but for Africa generally. He knew well that many thousands of people had been civilised and brought under the rule of noble and high-souled government—such as the Government of England was—and he was confident that these people, elevated from the condition of ignorance in which they now existed, would form, not communities of subject races merely, but integral parts of the grand whole of the British Colonial possessions. (Great cheering.)

Mr. VINTCENT (member of the Legislative Assembly, Cape of Good Hope), said he was in the same position as the previous speakers: he came to listen, and might say with truth he had been an attentive and also a gratified listener to the able and interesting paper with which they had been favoured. It was peculiarly gratifying to him, as a colonist only recently arrived, to find so much interest evinced on Colonial questions. It was a striking proof to him that there was a strong and mutual desire to draw the bond of union now existing between the mother-country and the Colonies still closer (hear, hear), to consolidate that Empire, which, though small in point of territory at home, was large when they took into consideration the large, important, and extensive Colonial territory which opened up all round. (Hear, hear). Mr. Donald Currie had been good enough to speak in hopeful and cheering terms of the future of Africa. He thanked him for the kind and encouraging tone in which he had spoken of that great, and he might say important continent, and trusted that his hopes might be realised—realised by the industry and by the enterprise of the colonists, and stimulated by cordial sympathy from the mother-country, and that those high and lofty views to which Mr. Donald Currie had referred so eloquently might be a guide for the future. (Hear, hear.) Whenever African matters were discussed the native question naturally always was prominently brought forward; and when that question was mentioned it was almost invariably called the "native difficulty." Now that term not inaptly expressed the condition of public opinion with reference to this difficult and intricate matter; but he might say that they at the Cape had been hitherto singularly fortunate in their native policy. For upwards of a quarter of a century the colonists at the Cape had lived in peace and security, and during that period neither the Imperial nor Colonial forces had been engaged in actual warfare on the immediate Colonial borders. During that time, too, the colonists had considerably increased in numbers and wealth, and large tracts of country which were previously occupied by restless tribes were now in the occupation of industrious and thriving farmers. That was also the case with the natives immediately bordering on the Colonial boundary. It was found that amongst those tribes many who formerly existed entirely by means of the chase and by raids into neighbouring districts, had now taken to tilling the soil and had become producers, and in consequence of their contact with white men had also been stimulated into habits of industry, and had acquired greater thrift and a strong desire to improve their position, the consequence being that there was a greater disposition among those natives to go into the Colony to supply that great want so often referred to—labour. (Hear, hear.) There had been a striking instance in connection with the railway works recently undertaken by the Cape Colony. When first those works began it was found impossible to get any of the natives beyond the border to engage for service on them. Now that had been quite changed, and he was informed a few days before his departure from the Cape by the Minister of Works, that he could get more Kafirs now than he could immediately employ on the works of the railway. (Hear, hear.) It was not only in this direction that improvement had taken place; but almost every year the Colonial boundaries were being extended, and frequent applications made to the local Legislature for the incorporation of certain tracts of land which had not been acquired by conquest or by forcing out the natives; but those incorporations took place in consequence of voluntary and spontaneous requests made by various native chiefs, and by their immediate followers, to be placed under the care and protection of the Colonial Government. He thought those two facts which he had mentioned were striking proofs that thus far the Colonial policy had not been without fruit. Now, it might be asked what the native policy was. Well, it was difficult to define, and, moreover, time would not permit him to do so that night; in the second place, it would be almost impossible strictly to define the native policy of the Cape, which was to a certain extent regulated and guided by circumstances, and by the condition of the different tribes with which they had to deal. He might say that the guiding principle which underlay all their intercourse and transactions with those tribes was as much as possible to obtain the confidence of the people—to gain their confidence by the strict justice of their rule, and also, after the annexation had been consented to and completed, as far as possible to reduce the power of the chiefs and to break up the tribal rights, and to endeavour to substitute Colonial magistrates and English laws for tribal laws and native customs. Those were the leading principles of the native policy of the Cape, which thus far he could say had been successful. In advocating that policy, which had been truly called a liberal policy, it must not be supposed, however, that he was advocating what was termed sometimes in the Colony "the Exeter Hall policy." He did not think it necessary there to describe that policy; it was one which he believed was dying out fast. Yet people were found here, most estimable, kind-hearted, well-meaning people, who to some extent very often looked upon the black man in every instance as an angel of light as compared with the Colonists, whom they too frequently viewed as relentless and cruel oppressors. He was happy to think that those views were no longer in the ascendant, as they were a little while ago; nor could he help thinking that if such opinions were held they were calculated to injure the natives themselves. They were cruel and unjust in the first place, because they not unnaturally exasperated the Colonists, and very often led them to commit acts which, as it were, were forced upon them by such injustice ; but, on the other hand, it was more cruel still towards the native, because it placed him in a false position, inflated him unduly, and rendered him proud and unmanageable ; and the consequence was that very often in self-defence the Colonists, who, it must be remembered, had long odds against them, were in some instances almost forced to wage what had been termed a war of extermination upon the poor natives. Now this we should wish and endeavour to avoid at the Cape of Good Hope. It certainly could not be the mission or the destiny of the white man to exterminate the coloured races, and if it was possible that the difficult and great problem could be solved in South Africa of utilizing the original races there it would be a great boon to all. He desired to make a few remarks on the subject of Confederation, although he had not nearly exhausted the subject of the native policy. Confederation was a great question, and so important as to require most mature consideration. He was rather struck by some remarks which he had heard that evening. They led him to believe that Confederation was already looked upon here as an accomplished fact, speakers having repeatedly spoken of "The Confederated States of South Africa." Now that, he thought, was not desirable. They, as colonists, would like to deal with the question in their own way and take their own time. Although they had been officially assured time after time that there was no desire whatever on the part of the Home Government to press this question upon them, still he could not help drawing his own conclusions from remarks heard that evening, which led him to believe that there was a tendency—though not actually expressed perhaps—but a strong tendency unduly to press this question upon the colonists, a thing he did not think it desirable should be done. When Confederation was spoken of they were constantly told that union was strength. There was no denying so patent a fact : union was certainly strength ; but then it should also be a true and perfect union (hear, hear), where the parts fitted well together, where they were not forced or squeezed together, but where they formed a compact whole. (Hear, hear.) Now, just look for a moment at the condition of South Africa. The Cape Colony had only for a few years enjoyed the rights of self-government. Only five years ago an important change was made in its constitution by the introduction of responsible government. That system was only now being successfully worked. The Cape Colony had, moreover, a revenue of a million and a half sterling. Now when they went to Natal they found a small Colony where the Constitution had been considerably curtailed of late by the action of the Home Government, while the revenue at present was very small compared with that of the Cape.' They next came to the Transvaal, now in a state of transition, with scarcely any revenue just now, and at present, he might say, under quasi-military rule. Then there was Griqualand West. That would soon be no more than a district, or what would be called in this country a county. Then there remained the Orange Free State, a small territory with a revenue

of about £100,000, or about a fifteenth portion of that of the
Cape of Good Hope. Now these provinces the Cape was at present
asked to confederate with ; and he put it to the meeting whether,
as a colonist of the Cape Colony, he was not justified in saying that
they certainly required a little time to consider before they threw
in their lot under a federal form of government with other States.
(Hear, hear.) He was strong in the view that union was certainly
desirable, and union would come before long ; but it often occurred
to him that they might very advantageously secure a yet more
perfect union than a confederation, and that was what he would
term a legislative union. (Cheers.) When the size of the Colony of
the Cape of Good Hope was taken into consideration, its improvement and wealth when compared with the other provinces, then he
thought it would be far more advantageous for all concerned to have
a legislative union, such as was originally contemplated when the
first Conference was held of the delegates of the North American
Colonies. He had not referred to the South African Permissive Bill
now passing through the British Parliament, because in the first
instance it was a strictly Permissive Bill, so that no Colony or
Province need accept any of its provisions, and in the second place
because important alterations had been made in the first draft Bill,
and which alterations he had not had an opportunity of considering,
and was therefore not prepared to express an opinion thereon.
He might, however, say that he did not believe that the Cape
Colony would accept any Bill which was calculated to curtail any of
the political privileges which it now enjoyed. The Cape Colonists
were truly loyal. He need not repeat that. Every British Colony
contained none but loyal subjects, but they were also British subjects,
and as such they valued and cherished their free representative
institutions. (Great cheering.)

Mr. LAMPORT, of Natal, said he should take the liberty to say
a few words, because there was on that map (pointing) a country
which had occupied a considerable share of the paper read, and
which country he happened to represent. He had been a colonist
for about twenty-seven years, and claimed to know something of
South Africa and the circumstances of that colony. He desired,
however, to say one word on behalf of Natal on one particular point,
and he took leave to preface it by remarking that, with respect to
the subject of the paper which had been read, he wished to impress
upon the meeting with more precision than had been done by the
essayist, one point. They would never do any good with the native
races, as regarded Natal, or as respected colonisation generally, until
they could offer at the outset protection and security. Without that
all would be perfectly in vain. He reminded them that Mr. Froude
had said that the native races could be counted almost by millions,
and that in the Colony of Natal 400,000 natives were present.
He had reminded them also that the adjoining country, Zulu Land,
that Cetchwayo had from 28,000 to 40,000 men under arms who
could be called upon immediately, who were under military training,
organised in regiments, and in readiness at a moment's notice. The

one point he (Mr. Lamport) would impress upon the meeting would be to use their influence with the Government to give it protection. He would fall back upon his experience and make good his position in this way. In Natal proper they had about 150,000 natives in their midst, and notwithstanding they had all those elements—those formidable people of the Zulu—it would scarcely be believed that after all the years that had elapsed, the British Government had only maintained in the Colony of Natal for their protection a paltry half-wing of a regiment. When the inadequacy of that protection was first tested an appeal took place three years ago under the terms of Langalibalele. The force at the command of the Government was utterly inadequate for the purpose; they simply had half a regiment, about 120 men all told, and could not move up 200 troops, not having the requisite force to back them up, and the Volunteers they could muster were something under 100 strong; and they only had two small field-pieces to go with them, all of which provoked from the natives manifestations of ridicule and contempt. He remembered a man remarking to him when this force marched through the streets of Zoelberg :—" They go, but they'll not come back again." In the lamentable affair with Langalibalele there were only about fifty Volunteers, and they dwindled down to forty-two. Therefore he would say that, before they could inspire a feeling of security, they must offer protection. It was true that, connected with that affair with Langalibalele, Sir Garnet Wolseley was sent out—whose name he respected—and he made painstaking inquiries in the Colony ; but it only resulted in their sending out another half-wing of a regiment. He remembered, also, that there was an agent sent out—a painstaking man—with General Cox to report on the defences of the Colony for the benefit of the war which Sir G. Wolseley was then carrying on. He was called upon to fill up a printed form as a justice of the peace, and he remembered sending in his report. He met Mr. Froude at Sir Garnet Wolseley's table and outside the Cathedral, and expressed to him those feelings in which all concurred, of the utter inadequacy of the Volunteer force to defend the place. Therefore it was the important duty of the British Government to maintain in those districts a force sufficient to inspire a sense of security. He heard it said that they must not depend upon England, but upon Volunteers, and the military force must be supplemented by colonisation, in which everyone from fourteen to sixty would be capable of bearing arms. He would say, as the result of his opinion, that Confederation was nothing. He had always described it as a piece of dilettanteness. They would never be able to get a council of men together, and they would be able to do nothing when they did get together. Had they concurred, and had there been Confederation, what would they do ? There there were two small Republics and half a regiment, which would have to be broken up into two—one for the Transvaal; then they would have left the British territory without any protection, which was carrying out the principle of *reductio ad absurdum*, leaving such a contemptible little force as would be no protection whatever. (Hear, hear.)

The PRESIDENT said: Ladies and gentlemen, I will only say a few words. I was greatly struck by the ability of Mr. Donald Currie's paper, especially from the local colouring that he had given it, although he has never been in the Colony. He touched on a vast number of points, which have led to a most interesting and instructive discussion. (Hear, hear.) Many of those points are of considerable importance; and perhaps I might suggest to Mr. Vintcent that no doubt the gentleman who talked of confederation as "being already accomplished" had been contemplating the great advantages that he hoped would follow on confederation, and had looked upon the prospect of such a thing in his mind's eye so long, that at last the wish became the father of the thought, and he fancied that that confederation perhaps may still be brought about, though Mr. Vintcent and also Mr. Lamport do not think it advisable to have it spoken of as if it were already *un fait accompli*. With regard to Mr. Trollope, who has said he was more practised with the pen than the tongue, we must thank him for having made an exception in our favour by addressing to us a most instructive speech. (Hear, hear.) I should have fancied, though he has been in the country, that he would have spoken in more favourable terms of the position and prospects of the Maori race. From what I have heard I thought they were showing a considerable amount of civilisation. Certainly there is nothing in the conduct of England or of the English settlers in New Zealand to lead to their annihilation and extinction; in fact, I have heard glowing accounts of the Maori women walking about the streets of the town in silk dresses and fashionable bonnets and smoking pipes with all the grace of French ladies. With regard to the Red Indians in North America, I am afraid our cousins over the line have not behaved with consideration to the Red Indians in their territory, but I believe in Canada they are not only well treated by the Government but by the settlers. The Government have, in the wisest and most far-seeing manner, settled them in communities on small territories of their own, and of which they are not allowed to dispose, and no man of the white race is allowed to settle amongst them. Even the Sioux, who have been in rebellion against the United States, take refuge on the British side of the borders, where, I believe, they often become quiet if not settled residents. (Hear, hear.) But certainly the question of the greatest importance was the one alluded to principally by Mr. Froude—that was the vast mass of natives, of able-bodied and intelligent men, that we have now to deal with, and the increasing number of whom we shall have to deal with as we progress on that continent, and also whose numbers will increase by the blessing of good government which we enforce upon those countries. It seems to me rather a terrible prospect. Mr. Vintcent held out hopes that they are acquiring civilisation and are working for their livelihood. When I was at the Cape, now some thirty-three years ago—no doubt things are much changed since then—but at that time nobody ever thought that a Kafir would work to better himself permanently. It was then said that the Kafir might work for a few shillings, and as soon as he got home he went back to a missionary station to live upon those shillings till they had gone; but I am glad to hear they are acquiring taste and habits of civilisation. Another point referred to was irrigation. That undoubtedly is most important for the Colony. I know that it has a rich soil, and that the strength of the sun dries it up till it is like a macadamized road, and it is utterly impossible to grow anything without showers, and yet there had been ample falls of rain, which, judiciously stored, would render the country fruitful. Colonel Crossman alluded to the difficulty about the capital. With respect to that, I do not think Cape Town need ever be afraid, even though it should not be the political capital, of losing its supremacy. From its geographical position, it must always be an important military station; and I hope our Government will also take the advice of Captain Colomb, and that the United Kingdom and the Colonies will undertake at some time to protect those important points he referred to in his able paper read here last meeting, by forming dockyards and by having the proper means of coaling and revictualling our ships of war, and fortifying such stations; and in that event Cape Town and Simon's Bay could not be neglected. With regard to Confederation and the annexation of the Transvaal, I was this afternoon looking at some Transvaal newspapers sent to me, and I gathered from them that the annexation seems to have gone off in the most satisfactory and successful way. (Hear, hear.) It appears that those who approve of the measure carefully avoid expressing any exultation that they might feel, so as to avoid giving offence to the other side. Those who object to it seem to accept it with very great resignation and with very little reluctance indeed. I beg now to offer our thanks to Mr. Donald Currie for the trouble he has taken in preparing his admirable paper. (Loud and prolonged cheering.)

Mr. DONALD CURRIE, in acknowledging the vote of thanks, said:—My Lord Duke, Ladies, and Gentlemen,—I feel highly gratified by the kind terms in which your Grace has proposed the thanks of the meeting. I would only add one word with respect to Mr. Vintcent's able remarks. If he had been present at the banquet which was given to Sir Bartle Frere before leaving for the Cape he would have heard from Lord Carnarvon that her Majesty's Government had no intention to interfere with the privileges of the colonists. The Confederation Bill is a Permissive Bill in its spirit and object. (Hear, hear.) It was sent to the Colonies and States of South Africa with the distinct intimation that they were to give their opinions upon its clauses. Many gentlemen here heard Lord Carnarvon express in the strongest terms possible that it was quite erroneous to suppose that he intended in any sense to curtail the liberty of the Colonists, or to take away their rights under responsible government. (Hear, hear.) As regards roads and the opening up of South Africa and Eastern and Central Africa, it was with the greatest pleasure I had the honour this afternoon, after my paper was finished, to receive from the Royal Geographical Society an intimation that they wished to open out roads from the South and from the Eastern side of Africa into the interior, and had arrangements in progress for an Exploration Fund. The Royal Geographical Society have appointed a Committee with the view to plan a systematic exploration from the different points on the coast, and we may look for the best results to that continent. (Applause.)

Mr. FREDERICK YOUNG (Hon. Secretary) announced that this meeting was the concluding one of the series for the present Session.

The company then separated.